The Silver Whistle

by JAY WILLIAMS

illustrated by FRISO HENSTRA

PARENTS' MAGAZINE PRESS

NEW YORK

Other books by Jay Williams

Stupid Marco
School for Sillies
The Practical Princess
The King with Six Friends
The Cookie Tree
The Question Box
Philbert the Fearful
co-author of the Danny Dunn *books*

For Ben and Jesse

01561

The Wise Woman of the West had a daughter whose name was Prudence. She was a cheerful girl, as wise as her name, and as homely as the day is long.

She had a snub nose, a wide mouth, straight straw-colored hair, and so many freckles that it looked as if someone had sprinkled her with cinnamon.

When the time came for the Wise Woman of the West to die, she called her daughter to her and said, "My dear, you must go out and make your way in the world. I can do nothing about your looks, but you have a merry heart and a lively mind, and there are plenty of people who like freckles. All that I have to give you is this silver whistle. If you blow it once, the birds will come to your call. If you blow it twice, the insects will be your friends. If you blow it three times, the beasts will speak to you. Thus you will never be lonely."

"Suppose I were to blow it four times?" asked Prudence. "Try not to do so," said her mother, gravely. "For if you do, it will make a sound shrill enough to shatter glass and the whistle will be broken."

So off Prudence went to make her way in the world, with nothing but the clothes on her back and the silver whistle in her pocket. She traveled for many a day and many a mile and at last she came to a house that stood on four legs in the middle of a wood. The house turned round to face her, and out came an old witch. She was as dry as a winter leaf, and had only a few brown teeth. "What do you want?" said she.

"I am making my way in the world," said Prudence. "Have you any work for me?"

"Plenty of work," cackled the witch. "And a silver penny on the first day of every month if you do whatever I ask."

"I don't mind," said Prudence. "It will make a nice change."

She became the witch's servant, and if the work was hard it was also interesting, for the witch did magic from morning to night and there were always plenty of vistors. Whenever Prudence was lonely, she blew her silver whistle and talked to a bird, a bee, or a beast.

One day, a messenger from the king came through the forest. He had a proclamation which he had been commanded to read in every corner of the kingdom. It said:

> On the thirty-first day of May,
> Prince Pertinel is to be married.
> Therefore, all the maidens of the
> land are to come to the palace so
> that the prince may choose the one
> who suits him best, to be his bride.
> Signed, King Quither V.

"Very good," said the witch. "I have a mind to be chosen. For there is nothing I'd like better than to be a princess, and someday queen."

"Dear me," said Prudence, and she couldn't help chuckling. "It seems to me that you would have even less of a chance than I, for if I am homely you are perfectly hideous."

"So you think," retorted the witch. "But with the magical mirror of Morna I will win the prince's heart. For whoever looks into that mirror becomes more beautiful than the dawn of a spring morning. The spell lasts as long as the mirror lasts, and that will be long enough for me."

"And have you the mirror of Morna?" asked Prudence.

"No," said the witch. "But you are going to get it for me."

"I am? Where is it, and how shall I get it?"

"It is kept in the treasure house of The Wazar," the witch said. "And I don't know how you are going to get it. But however you get it, it must be given to you freely or its magic will not work."

"That doesn't make things any easier," murmured Prudence. "Where is the treasure house of The Wazar?"

"I don't know that either," said the witch. "All I know is that it is far to the south, in a land where the trees have leaves but no branches and where the ground moves when the wind blows."

"I have never heard of such a place," Prudence said.

"Well, are you going?"

"I don't mind," said Prudence. "It will make a nice change."

She packed up a loaf and a piece of cheese in her handkerchief and put her silver whistle in her pocket. Then she said to the witch, "By the way, what exactly is a Wazar?"

"Nobody knows," said the witch. "I wish you luck."

Off went Prudence, traveling south under the great trees of the forest. She wandered for many days. She was chilled by the wind and wetted by the rain. Sometimes she rested at inns or in the cottages of farmers. Sometimes she ate nothing but dry bread for her dinner and slept on the hard ground. Whenever she felt lonely, she blew her whistle and talked to a bird, a bee, or a beast. She remained as cheerful as she could, and journeyed on, looking for a land where the trees had leaves but no branches and where the ground moved when the wind blew.

After a time, she climbed a steep mountain and came down its other side into a wide plain. The sun blazed overhead. There were tall trees with rough, scaly trunks and from their tops grew large graceful leaves like bunches of feathers. Underfoot, the ground was soft sand, and when the wind blew, the sand stirred and shifted.

"Ah," said Prudence. "This must be the land of The Wazar."

Not far away was a magnificent palace built of white marble. There were a thousand windows in its high walls. From a hundred spires and domes flew banners of red and gold. Prudence walked to the palace and stood before the gates.

They were wide open.

"I suppose that means I can go in," she said.

She entered and found herself in a large hall. It was splendidly furnished but everything was covered with dust. Spiderwebs hung from the ceiling. No servant came forward, and no guard stopped her. All was empty, silent, and dirty.

She passed through it into a corridor. She found a number of fine rooms, and all were as empty and as untended as the first. In the last room, seated on a chair studded with diamonds was a fat moon-faced man. He wore a tall red hat with a diamond on the front of it. His robes were embroidered with golden threads. Although the chair didn't look very comfortable, he was sound asleep with his hands clasped on his round stomach.

Prudence cleared her throat. "Good day," she said.

He opened one eye and then the other.

"I am looking for The Wazar," she said.

"Then you can stop looking and go away," said the man, closing his eyes again.

"Why do they call you *The* Wazar?" asked Prudence.

His eyes snapped open and he sat up. "Because I am the only one there is," he answered. "Why do you want to know?"

"I'm curious. What is a Wazar?"

"I am, of course. And now that we're asking questions, who are you and what are you doing here?"

"My name is Prudence. I'm making my way through the world," said she. The Wazar stroked his ginger-colored whiskers. "Hm," he said. "I don't suppose you're looking for a job, are you? All my servants have run off and left me."

"I don't mind," said Prudence. "It will make a nice change. Why did your servants leave you?"

"It is surprising, isn't it?" said The Wazar. "I am one of the kindest, most generous men imaginable. I suppose they were frightened because my neighbor, Arbroag the Unpleasant, has threatened to destroy me."

"Why should he do that?"

"Well," said the Wazar, "we Wazars, as you know, are fond of diamonds. And since I am the only Wazar there is, I am even fonder of them than any-one. I stole a tiny little diamond from Arbroag–it only weighed about forty pounds–and when he demanded it back, I told him in the quietest and friendliest way that he was a thick-headed pig-snouted ring-tailed guttersnipe. For some reason he became very angry and put a curse on me."

"I see," said Prudence. "When does he plan to destroy you?"

"Tonight," said The Wazar, gloomily. "And I haven't even had my dinner."

"Goodness!" said Prudence. "It doesn't sound as though a job with you would last very long."

"If you will work for me until sunrise tomorrow," said The Wazar, "and help me to escape from Arbroag's curse, I will give you whatever you wish from my treasure house. However," he added, quickly, "you must let *me* choose what it shall be."

Prudence laughed. "Very well," she said. "What do you want me to do first?"

"First of all," said The Wazar, folding his hands over his stomach again, "clean up the palace. It's a mess."

Prudence looked about for a broom.

"Oh, I forgot to mention," said The Wazar, "that part of the curse Arbroag put on me was that here no broom will sweep and no mop will mop. Now, you'd better get busy."

For a moment, Prudence stood in thought. Then she took out her silver whistle and blew a blast on it.

In a twinkling, the air was full of birds. Hundreds and thousands of them came, flapping and chirping.

Their wings blew away the dust. The larger birds picked up the bigger bits of rubbish; the smaller ones took grains of dirt or spiderwebs. Then they flew off, and when they had gone the palace was clean.

The Wazar pointed to one feather which remained on the floor. "Not very neat," he said. "And the noise of the birds has given me a headache. Now I'd like some dinner."

He led Prudence to the kitchen. But before she could begin to cook, it grew dark. It was not the darkness of night, but a deeper darkness as if every light everywhere in the world had been blown out. The Wazar's teeth could be heard chattering.

"I can't bear this," he groaned. "Do something!"
Prudence tried to light a candle. But although it
flamed up, it gave off only a tiny glow, like the
faint glimmer of a distant star.
"I forgot to tell you," said The Wazar, "that part of
the curse Arbroag put on me was that when the
darkness comes no lamp nor candle will give light."
Prudence took out her silver whistle and blew two
blasts on it. At once, millions of fireflies came from
the desert. They swarmed in at the windows and
hung in clusters in the air. All their shining bodies
together were like bright moonlight.

Prudence soon had a fire going in the stove and was able to cook a fine stew. The Wazar wrapped his robe about him, sat down at the kitchen table and ate with a hearty appetite.

"It's not exactly what I'm used to," he complained. "I would have preferred roast pheasant, sugared rose petals, and champagne. However, I suppose this is the best you can do."

Prudence thought she could understand why all his servants had left him. She said nothing, however, but helped herself to some stew.

Then it began to grow cold. Frost formed on the windows and walls. Icicles hung glittering from the rafters. And the flames of the fire in the stove froze and stood fixed as if they were made of yellow glass.

"I forgot to tell you," whispered The Wazar, "that part of the curse Arbroag put on me was that when the cold comes no flame nor fire will warm me. This is the end. Good-bye."

"Nonsense!" said Prudence. "You hired me to save you and that's what I intend to do."

She took out her silver whistle and blew three blasts on it.

In at the door bounded a lion.

The lion uttered a roar, and out by the other door bounded The Wazar. The lion ran after him. All through the palace they went, in one room and out the other, up stairs and down, and every time The Wazar stopped to catch his breath the lion would snarl and chase him again.

He grew hot from running. Sweat dripped down his face and stained his robe, and his cheeks were redder than his hat.

When at last the sun rose, he was thinner than he had been but warm and still alive.

"Now," said Prudence, "it is sunrise and I have done as you asked."

"That's true," said The Wazar, peevishly, "but I have lost ten pounds and I've had no sleep. However, I forgive you, for as I told you I am a kind and generous man. Come along with me to my treasure house."

The treasure house was heaped high with The Wazar's collection of diamonds. Diamonds of all shapes, colors and sizes lay there in dazzling heaps.

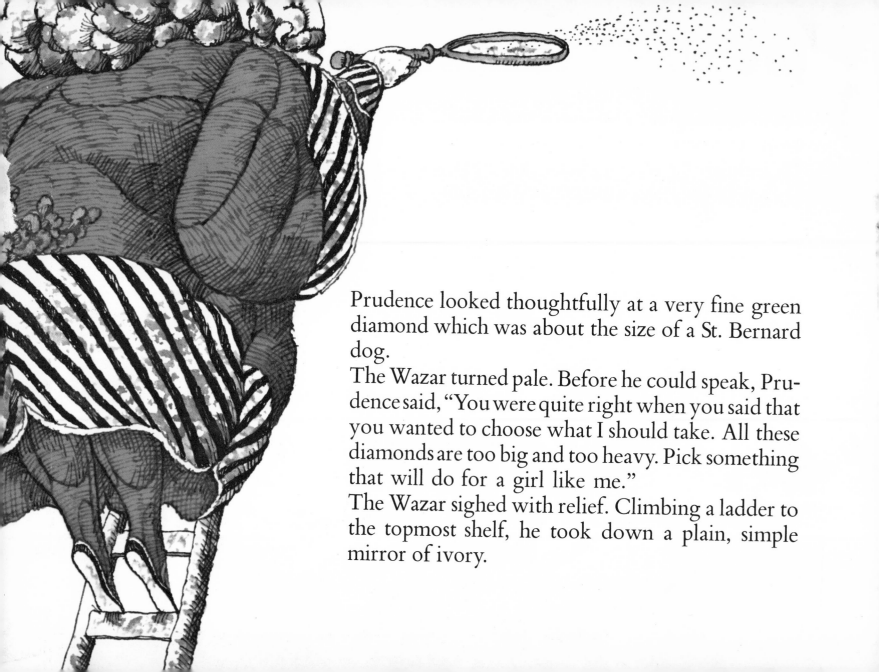

Prudence looked thoughtfully at a very fine green diamond which was about the size of a St. Bernard dog.

The Wazar turned pale. Before he could speak, Prudence said, "You were quite right when you said that you wanted to choose what I should take. All these diamonds are too big and too heavy. Pick something that will do for a girl like me."

The Wazar sighed with relief. Climbing a ladder to the topmost shelf, he took down a plain, simple mirror of ivory.

"This is the magical mirror of Morna," he said, blowing the dust off it. "It is said to make people beautiful. It's no use to me, as I'm already as beautiful as possible. But it might do you some good."

"You are right," said Prudence. "Do you give it to me freely?"

"Absolutely," said The Wazar, and he pushed her out the door and locked it behind him with sixteen keys.

Prudence started for home. When she had gone a mile or two, she thought, perhaps I might just take a peep into the mirror and see if it makes me beautiful. She was beginning to unwrap it, and then she laughed.

"I don't think I want to be beautiful," she said. "I might be different outside but I'd be the same inside, and I'm used to me the way I am. Anyway, I don't own the mirror, for I only got it for the witch." So she wrapped it up again and went on her way, as cheerfully as ever. When she came, at last, to the witch's house, it was the thirty-first of May. The witch came out screeching with impatience, and even the house hopped from foot to foot.

"High time you returned, you lazy thing!" she
screamed.
"Bring the mirror and follow me. We must hurry to
the king's palace."
The city was full of girls. They crowded the streets
and crammed the squares. Smiling, they went in
through the front door of the palace. Sadly, they filed
out through the back door.
When Prudence and the witch arrived, there were
only a few girls waiting to enter, for it was nearly
evening. At the door of the palace, the witch held out
her hand. Prudence gave her the mirror.

The witch gazed into it. Instantly, she straightened and grew taller. Her white hair turned to gold. Her face changed and she became so beautiful that all the birds began to sing as if it were the dawn of a spring morning. Into the palace she went, with Prudence behind her. There sat the king and queen, and before them stood Prince Pertinel. He was a tall, handsome young man but pale with weariness, and his eyes were glazed from the sight of so many maidens.

Prudence looked at the prince and then she looked at the witch. Although the witch's face was lovely, her eyes had not changed. They were old and hard, and full of witchcraft. She was different outside but the same inside.

"He must not marry her," Prudence said to herself. "If someday she becomes queen, she will be full of wickedness."

There was no help for it. With a sigh, Prudence took out her silver whistle and blew four blasts on it.

With the last note, the whistle split in two. But the mirror cracked with a loud noise and shattered to bits. And as the pieces clattered to the floor, the witch changed again into her own shape. With a yell of rage, she flew straight up into the air and vanished through the ceiling, leaving a large and untidy hole in the plaster.

Prince Pertinel stepped forward and took Prudence by the hand.

"Marvelous!" he said. "You are the girl for me."

Prudence stared at him in surprise.

"Me? But I'm not beautiful," she said.

The prince smiled. "That is true," he said. "But I never said I would choose the most beautiful girl in the kingdom. I said I would choose the one who suited me best. As it happens, I prefer freckles. Will you marry me?"

"Oh, well, I don't mind," said Prudence, returning his smile. "It will make a nice change."

R

EXTREME VENOM

BLACKBIRCH PRESS

An imprint of Thomson Gale, a part of The Thomson Corporation

THOMSON

GALE

Detroit • New York • San Francisco • San Diego • New Haven, Conn. • Waterville, Maine • London • Munich

THOMSON

★

GALE
™

Photo credits: Cover: all Corel Corporation except top left © PhotoDisc; top right © Jeffrey L.
Rotman/CORBIS; all pages © Discovery Communications, Inc., except for pages 1, 4, 12, 20, 24
Corel Corporation; page 8 © Joe McDonald/CORBIS; page 16 © PhotoDisc; page 28 © Jeffrey L.
Rotman/CORBIS; page 31 CDC/B.Thomason/PHIL; page 32 © Jonathan Blair/CORBIS; page 36 ©
Photos.com; page 40 © Karen Trist/Lonely Planet Images

LIBRARY OF CONGRESS CATALOGING-IN-PUBLICATION DATA
Venom / John Woodward, book editor.
    p. cm. — (Planet's most extreme)
  Includes bibliographical references and index.
  ISBN 1-4103-0392-6 (hardcover : alk. paper) — ISBN 1-4103-0434-5 (paper cover : alk.
paper)
    1. Poisonous animals—Juvenile literature. I. Woodward, John, 1958–. II. Series.

  QL100.V46 2005
  591.6'5—dc22

                                                                            2004019493

Printed in the United States of America
10 9 8 7 6 5 4 3 2 1

What is the deadliest animal on Earth? We're counting down the top ten most extreme venoms in the animal kingdom, and finding out just what happens when venom is taken to The Most Extreme.

10

The **Stingray**

Our countdown begins in warm waters around the world. Hiding in the shallows is the animal that's number ten in our countdown of extreme venom: the stingray. Each year in America alone, 50 times more people are injured by encounters with stingrays than with sharks! That's because we don't see them buried in the sand. If you stand on one, that whiplike tail lashes out and buries a venomous spine in your leg! It's a nasty surprise for even the biggest hunters in the sea.

For a hungry orca, a stingray is a mouth-watering morsel. But the stingray's sting contains not only enzymes that destroy flesh, but also serotonin, which causes instant excruciating pain. It's enough to make even these hungry hunters think twice!

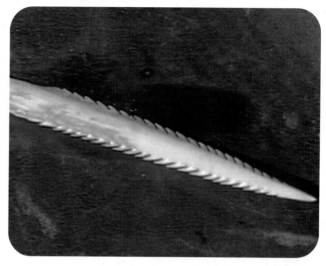

Be careful when you walk on the beach. You wouldn't want a close encounter with the stinger on a stingray's tail.

So why would anyone want to keep stingrays in a touch tank? At the Aquarium of the Pacific in Long Beach, California, even expert Mark Loos is cautious. Most of the time stingrays are peaceful, even playful animals. Some have called them the "pussycats of the sea." But if they get frightened, one flick of that muscular tail is enough to drive home their venomous spine. So Loos has a simple way of making stingrays harmless. He explains:

> *We're going to clip the stinger from the stingray. It doesn't actually hurt the animal. Because the stinger is made of keratin, it's like clipping fingernails. We're doing it to make sure that nobody accidentally gets stung. The stingers have the potential to grow back with venom, so every three months we gather up all the animals to make sure they don't have any stingers on them. Any that have grown back, we reclip.*

5

The stingray's venomous barb can be driven in so deep that it punctures your heart. Back in 1978, it was a very different poisoned puncture wound that hit the headlines. The city of London was home to Bulgarian dissident Georgi Markov, an outspoken protester against the Communist regime in his homeland. One day when he was waiting at a bus stop, he failed to notice a man behind him carrying an umbrella. Suddenly, he felt a stinging pain on the back of his right thigh. It's thought that a Bulgarian state security agent stabbed Markov with a most unusual umbrella. Markov never knew that his mortal illness was actually caused by the puncture wound. It was only

Imagine meeting a stingray on land! That's what happened to Georgi Markov in 1978, when an assassin stabbed him with a poisoned umbrella.

In order to avoid trouble, it's best to just stay clear of the stingray and its venomous tail (right).

after the autopsy that doctors discovered that the umbrella had inserted a tiny poison pellet into Markov's leg. The pellet contained ricin, a poison that is derived from the beans of the castor oil plant and 100 times as deadly as cobra venom.

Stingray venom may not be as lethal as ricin, but you still have to be careful of that stinger. Treat this venomous creature with respect and it won't attack.

The **Platypus**

When early European explorers traveled to faraway lands, they discovered new worlds with strange animals. But no animal was as bizarre as the creature that's coming in at number nine in our venomous countdown. It's the platypus.

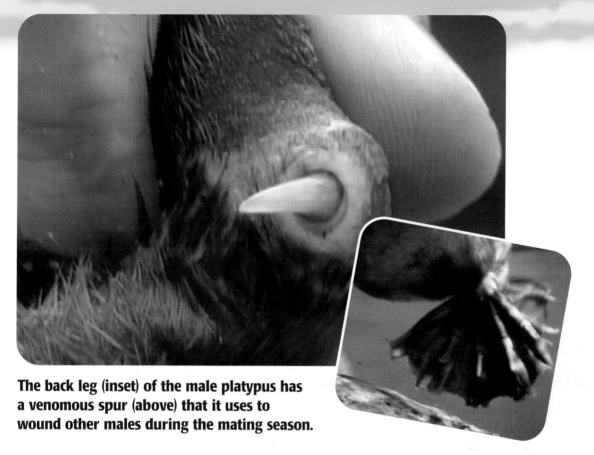

The back leg (inset) of the male platypus has a venomous spur (above) that it uses to wound other males during the mating season.

This animal lays eggs like a hen, yet it's covered with fur like a cat. It's got the tail of a beaver and the webbed feet of a swan. Add the bill of a duck and you get this furry collection of animal leftovers.

According to aboriginal legend, the first platypus was born after a young female duck mated with a water rat. The resulting creature has one feature that's not found in birds or mammals. The male platypus has a sharp spur on his hind leg that injects venom from a gland in his thigh. This venom can kill a dog or leave a human in agony. Since the venom is only secreted by mature males during the breeding season, its main target is usually other males looking to fight for territory.

The platypus wasn't the only discovery of the early explorers to be greeted with suspicion. When European sailors returned home from South America with a strange plant related to the deadly nightshade family, most people assumed that its bright red fruit would be poisonous. It wasn't until 1830 in America that Colonel Robert Johnson proved them wrong. When he announced he would eat a basket of the deadly fruit, a crowd of 2,000 watched him commit what they thought would be public suicide. Although the band played a somber tune,

In 1830 Colonel Robert Johnson ate a basketful of tomatoes to prove the fruit isn't poisonous. Would you eat pizza if tomatoes could kill?

With its beaverlike tail, webbed feet, and duck bill, the platypus sure looks like a science experiment gone bad, doesn't it?

Johnson didn't die. In fact, he reported that the fruit was delicious. He became rich selling the fruit—tomatoes! Today the average American eats more than 22 pounds of tomatoes each year.

While the image of the tomato has changed, the platypus is still considered to be one of the world's strangest animals. However, it could have been made even stranger if that lonely duck of aboriginal legend had mated with the next contender in the countdown.

8

The Gila Monster

To round up number eight in our countdown of extreme venom, mosey on down to see Chris Reimann on his ranch in Comfort, Texas. It pays to be careful here, for his little dawgies are real monsters. Meet the real Gila monster. Chris Reimann runs the Gila Ranch, which is home to about 100 Gila monsters. He believes that his lizards don't deserve their reputation as monsters.

The Gila gets its bad reputation because its bite really is worse than its bark. This monster is number eight in the count-down because it's one of only two venomous lizards in the world. If you're bitten by a Gila, it clamps on in a vise grip as its razor-sharp teeth slice open your flesh. Then modified sali-vary glands produce venom that dribbles down the teeth and deep into the wound. The more the monsters chew, the more venomous saliva they deliver, with terrifying results. Chris Reimann describes what it's like:

Although Chris Reimann knows firsthand how painful the bite of the Gila monster is, he loves to handle the venomous lizards.

When I was bit, the first few minutes I felt nausea and a little pain from the bite. Then I had a lymph node that was throbbing a bit, then my hand was throbbing, then my back started to hurt, then it went to my chest. I became worried, so I went to the hospital. I was vomiting, had cold sweats, and an erratic heartbeat.

Thanks to quick medical treatment, Chris survived this venomous encounter. Surprisingly, he has no hard feelings!

It's ironic that the unforgettable bite of a Gila monster may one day actually help people to remember. Scientists have analyzed Gila venom and created an experimental drug that works in the human brain. There's a chemical in Gila spit that acts on the receptor pathways in the brain that affect memory. Chemical companies are hoping that their new drug could help reduce the symptoms of memory

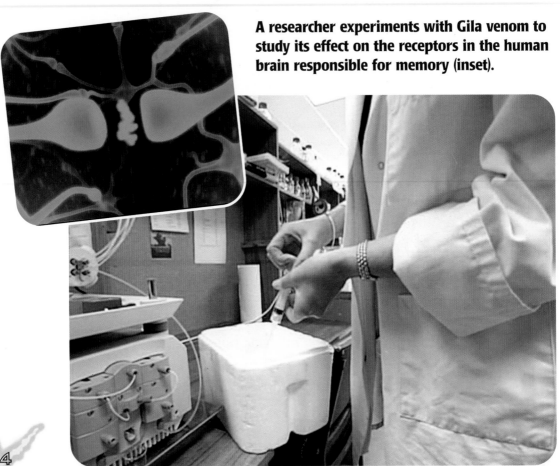

A researcher experiments with Gila venom to study its effect on the receptors in the human brain responsible for memory (inset).

Who would've ever guessed that spit from a Gila monster could help the human brain to function?

loss for the millions of sufferers of Alzheimer's disease. Memories are made up of many things, and one of them could soon be Gila monster spit.

The **Bee**

The next contender in our countdown of extreme venom is the bee. Bees have buzzed their way into number seven in the countdown because for some people, these tiny insects really are the most lethal creatures in the world, even though each one only carries little more than a millionth of an ounce of venom.

A bee sinks its barbed stinger into the skin of a victim (above). As protection from painful stings, a beekeeper wears special gear (inset).

When you're stung by a bee, venom is pumped through the barbed sting into the skin, where the chemical melittin works on the nerve endings of pain receptors, causing a brief burst of agony. For one person in a thousand, however, bee venom causes an allergic reaction not just in the skin, but in other parts of the body, including the vital organs. If left untreated, the patient can die of anaphylactic shock in less than five minutes! No wonder most people dealing with bees on a daily basis wear protective clothing.

17

Some people in Waldorf, Maryland, however, uncover themselves for bees. Here, people actually want to be stung for the good of their health! This is bee venom therapy in action. The theory is that in addition to causing pain, the bee sting also heals.

Bee venom therapy changed the life of Pat Wagner. In 1992, multiple sclerosis had reduced her to what she called "a bedridden, breathing corpse." Now, more than 45,000 stings later, she is able to walk again and lead a normal life.

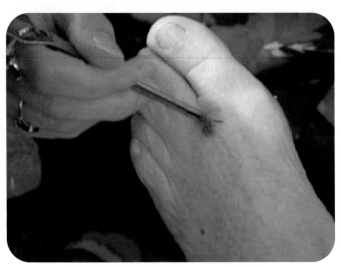

Some people think bee venom is good for their health. Nothing like a bee sting in your hand and foot to get the blood flowing!

Known as the Bee Lady, Pat Wagner often stings herself with bee venom, which contains a strong anti-inflammatory agent.

Researchers believe that the chemical melittin is a powerful anti-inflammatory substance. Wagner is now known as the Bee Lady, and she happily shares her therapy with people from all over the world. She describes amazing results from the therapy:

> *I have seen so many miracles when I sting people—*
> *just absolute miracles. Apitherapy is phenomenal.*

6

The **Scorpion**

It may sound too good to be true, but the next contender may also save people's lives with the sting in its tail. In California's Palm Desert, there are two ways to find the scorpion. You can poke around under rocks and hope you get lucky. Or you can wait until nightfall and go hunting with an ultraviolet lamp.

A scorpion looks very menacing in ultraviolet light (above). If that's not enough to scare you, the venom oozing from its tail (inset) should be!

Nobody's sure why the scorpion glows under ultraviolet light, but everybody knows why it's number six in the countdown. In 1999, more than 13,000 Americans were stung by scorpions. Few stings were fatal, thanks to good medical care, but in Mexico, scorpions are estimated to kill 1,000 people a year!

How would you like to be locked in a box with nearly 3,500 scorpions? Meet Kanchana Ketkeaw from Thailand. She spent a world record 32 days inside a glass cage with 3,400 venomous scorpions. She was stung nine times, but the venom had little effect on her because she'd developed immunity during seven years of performing with the lethal creatures.

Few people would attempt to break the record set by Kanchana Ketkeaw, who spent 32 days in a cage filled with scorpions.

Pucker up! Ketkeaw can kiss this scorpion without fear because she's developed immunity to scorpion venom.

There may be another reason why scorpion attacks are not always fatal. Recent research suggests that the scorpion can set its venom on either stun or kill. Instead of wasting venom on self-defense, it uses a pre-venom that causes extreme pain. It's a clever strategy because the deadly true venom is a complex cocktail of proteins that's expensive to make.

5 The **Stonefish**

To find the next contender in our venomous countdown, take a trip to a tropical island in the Pacific. Walk next to a coral reef and you could think you're in paradise, even though your next step could be your last. These waters are home to the world's most venomous fish: the stonefish.

Did that rock just move? It's actually a stonefish gobbling up a fish it killed with its poisonous spines (right).

When it's feeding time at the Aquarium of the Pacific in Long Beach, California, Christine Light keeps well clear of the animal that's lurking at number five in the countdown. The reason the stonefish is so dangerous is that it looks like a stone.

Stonefish actually use their venom as a defense mechanism. They have 12 to 14 dorsal spines, which are covered in a thick skin layer. When they're sitting on the bottom, their dorsal spines will be lying flat against their body. But if they're provoked, the spines come up and the skin pulls away from the spines. When the spines penetrate someone's foot or limb, the pressure causes the venom to shoot up into the person or fish they're attacking.

Sharing a meal with a fish can be deadly, but for some people, that's part of the attraction. Manhattan's Nippon restaurant serves not stonefish, but puffer fish. Gourmets come to try a dish called fugu, a delicacy that means instant death if not properly prepared. It contains a poison that's 275 times deadlier than cyanide! It's concentrated in the ovaries, intestines, and liver of the fish, which all have to be carefully removed, because a lethal dose would fit on a pinhead!

The active ingredient is tetradoxin —a chemical that attacks the nervous system, paralyzing the muscles of the body. Sometimes it can cause a coma almost indistinguishable from death. And that's why some researchers believed that tetradoxin could also be used to create the living dead!

This man seems a bit nervous about his lunch, and with good reason. There's a chance his food is full of lethal puffer fish venom.

In Haiti, it is believed that people can be brought back from the grave as zombies. Researchers have suggested that sorcerers grind up puffer fish as part of their magic powder. In 1962, when a voodoo victim was rushed to the hospital unable to breathe, doctors signed the man's death certificate. Yet twenty years later, the same man can visit the cemetery to see his own grave. Clervius Narcisse believes he emerged from his grave as a zombie slave.

Clervius Narcisse believes he came back from the dead as a zombie after he was drugged with ground-up puffer fish.

Drugged by a voodoo sorcerer's magic powder, Narcisse was unable to move as he witnessed his own funeral. The next thing he remembers is being taken from the grave to become a slave. He claims to have worked on a farm for two years, until one day the overseer failed to correctly administer the sorcerer's drug. Narcisse was released from his zombie state and returned to the living, including his surprised family.

Step on a stonefish and you're in for an even bigger surprise. This ugly monster may pack a powerful punch, but it's no match for our next contender—a tiny terror with a really mean mouth!

4 The **Octopus**

There's a sea monster lurking off the coast of Australia. Our next contender couldn't sink a ship, but these tranquil waters are home to a killer with a bite that packs enough venom to kill ten people. It's stealthy and the size of a golf ball. At number four in the countdown is the blue ringed octopus!

It's not hard to see how it got its name, but those infamous blue rings only really light up as a warning when the animal feels threatened. Unfortunately, some people are attracted to the pretty colors and pick up the cute little octopus. This is a big mistake. Its bite is so small that many victims don't even realize they've been wounded, let alone injected with a neurotoxin 10,000 times more deadly than cyanide! It's a venom that paralyzes humans and potential prey.

The blue rings (close-up, inset) on this octopus might look pretty, but they're actually a warning to others to back off.

The venom is part of the octopus's spit and is produced in two glands as big as its brain. The octopus hunts crabs either by spitting out a cloud of the toxic saliva, or by jumping its prey and biting through a chink in the crab's armored shell.

Strangely enough, the octopus doesn't make its own venom. Dense colonies of bacteria actually produce the deadly neurotoxins. They live safely tucked away in the octopus's salivary glands.

Could you stomach this cook's food? He blows his nose without washing his hands, he sneezes right into his palm, and he's working with an open sore.

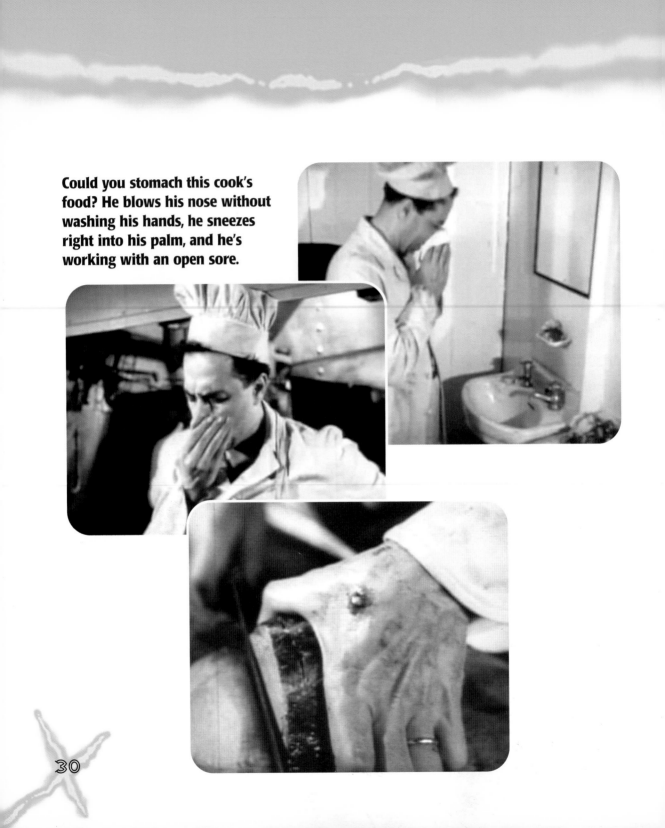

In addition to being gross, the cook's bad hygiene could spread deadly salmonella bacteria (right) into your food.

Harmful bacteria can live in all kinds of places, including our kitchens. Some kitchens can be breeding grounds for the bugs that cause food poisoning. This year there's a one in four chance that you'll become sick thanks to bacteria like salmonella or listeria. Food poisoning is likely to kill 9,000 Americans this year. That's why you don't want a cook with poor personal hygiene or a dirty kitchen.

3

The Cone Snail

The next contender in our countdown of extreme venom is a truly deadly snail. The slowest assassin in the world lives inside a shell. It may look harmless, but the cone snail can kill as quickly as lightning.

A cone snail injects deadly venom into a fish with its needle (above). The snail finishes off the fish by sucking it through its feeding tube (inset).

When it moves at top speed, the only thing it could hope to catch would be a rock. That's why it has had to develop a more clever hunting technique. It is armed with a hypodermic needle full of venom.

The cone snail moves too slowly to get more than one chance to paralyze its prey, so the venom has to kill quickly. At least 30 people have been killed by cone snails. University of Utah biologist Baldomero Olivera tried to find out why this venom is so powerful:

We discovered that when they inject their venom they're not just injecting a few toxins. They're injecting a complicated cocktail of 50 or 100 different components, and each of them is like a drug. Cone

A cone snail shoots its needle toward an unsuspecting fish. The snail's venom contains a large number of lethal toxins.

**Could the cone snail actually help people?
Clinical trials have shown that its venom
contains a very powerful painkiller.**

*snail venom changes the way the nervous system acts. Its
components may become among the most effective painkillers and
drugs against epilepsy and mental illness.*

Clinical trials have found a cone snail painkiller is a thousand times
more effective than morphine, without the nasty side effects. While
the cone snail may one day provide a cure for human pain, this
slow-motion assassin will always give fish a real headache.

2 The **Sea Snake**

We've had nothing but trouble from the next contender since the beginning of time. A serpent got Adam and Eve kicked out of the Garden of Eden, and some snakes are still bad news today. That's why the snake slithers in at number two in the countdown, especially those living in this underwater Eden off the Australian coast.

Sea snake venom is one of the most potent in the world. A single drop is reputed to be able to kill three men. That's why researchers like Dr. Bryan Fry of the Australian Venom Research Unit find them so irresistible. The venom of every snake species has its own chemical formula. The more you know about the formula, the better the antivenin, or antidote, you can make. The tricky part is getting the venom out of the snake!

Milking the snake to extract its venom is the first step in the process of creating antivenin. Small doses of the venom get the immune system to produce antibodies, molecules that can knock the venom off the victim's nerve cells. You have to get the antivenin to the patient quickly, however.

Although most people would swim away from a sea snake as fast as they could, Dr. Bryan Fry loves to catch sea snakes and milk them for venom (bottom).

Miami, Florida, is home to the world's only emergency antivenin response unit. Captain Al Cruz and Ernie Jillson are the men of Venom One. Run by the Miami-Dade Fire Department, Venom One provides a lifeline for snakebite victims. Established in 1998, it now has the most extensive antivenin collection in the United States, covering 95 percent of the world's venomous snakes. Captain Al Cruz explains the risks of having venomous snakes as pets:

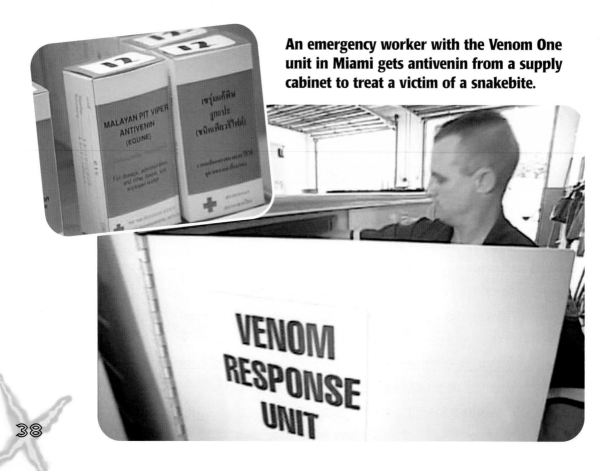

An emergency worker with the Venom One unit in Miami gets antivenin from a supply cabinet to treat a victim of a snakebite.

With his bitten arm in a sling, a snakebite victim receives the antivenin that will save his life.

When someone keeps a venomous snake, they need to understand that it's not a matter of if you're going to get bit, it's a matter of when. We have an assortment of antivenins that is a lifeline for people not only locally but also nationally. You might only need one vial of antivenin, yet with a king cobra you might need forty. What makes Venom One unique and makes it work so well is that you call one number and we respond. We've treated over 500 bites in the last four years with not a single fatality.

The Box Jellyfish

For seven months of every year, a nearly invisible killer makes the sea a deadly playground and clears some of the best beaches in Australia. The only safe place to swim is within the shelter of a fine mesh net. Venture outside the net and you're playing Russian roulette with the animal with The Most Extreme venom in the countdown: the box jellyfish.

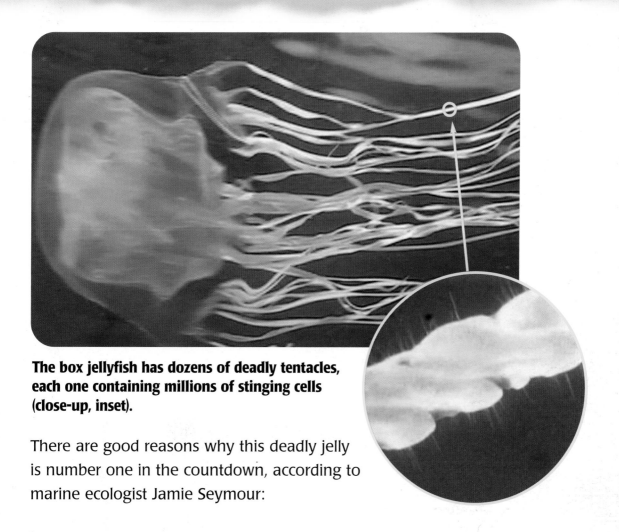

The box jellyfish has dozens of deadly tentacles, each one containing millions of stinging cells (close-up, inset).

There are good reasons why this deadly jelly is number one in the countdown, according to marine ecologist Jamie Seymour:

> *These animals are the most venomous animals in the world. There is absolutely no doubt about that at all. There have been recorded instances where people have had six or seven feet worth of tentacles on their body and it's killed them. A full-grown animal has 15 tentacles on each corner, a total of 60 tentacles, and each one of those tentacles is probably seven to eight feet long. One animal has the potential to kill 60 people. And he can do it within minutes.*

When an unsuspecting victim blunders into the almost invisible jellyfish, the agony is instant. People say it's like being branded with red-hot irons, and that's just what the scars look like.

Unsuspecting swimmers get too close to a jellyfish. Its stingers leave scars (inset) that look like they were made with red-hot irons.

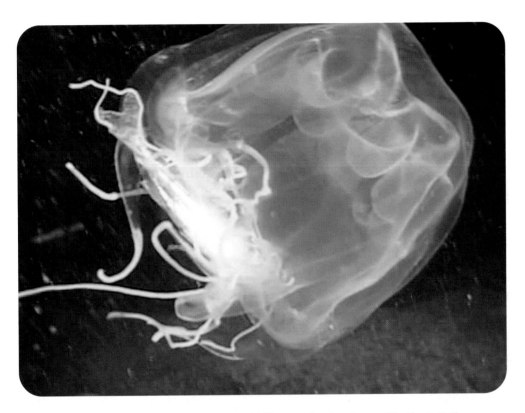

Jellyfish tentacles are covered with billions of stinging cells that deliver powerful poison at the slightest touch.

The jellyfish is number one in the countdown because those trailing tentacles are covered in 4 billion stinging cells. At the slightest touch, the cells blast a microscopic harpoon through your skin to inject its incredibly powerful neurotoxin. But the jellyfish doesn't hunt humans. It has smaller fish to fry. Its venom is so extreme because it has to paralyze fish quickly, before their struggles snap the tentacles.

43

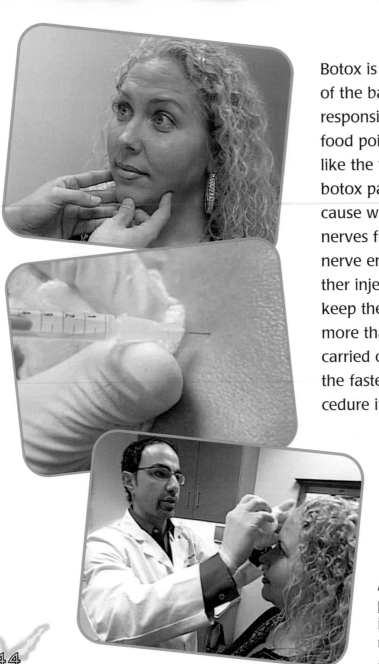

Botox is actually a purified form of the bacterial neurotoxin responsible for the most deadly food poisoning in the world. Just like the venom of a jellyfish, botox paralyzes the muscles that cause wrinkles by preventing the nerves from firing. Eventually the nerve endings regenerate, so further injections are required to keep the wrinkles at bay. With more than 1.6 million procedures carried out every year, botox is the fastest-growing cosmetic procedure in America today.

A woman has botox, a powerful poison, injected into her forehead to keep unsightly wrinkles from appearing.

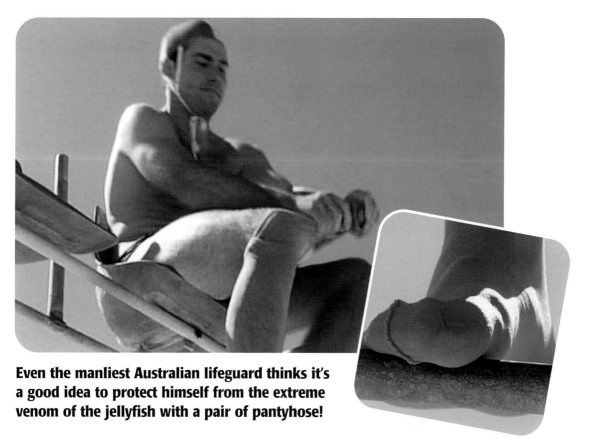

Even the manliest Australian lifeguard thinks it's a good idea to protect himself from the extreme venom of the jellyfish with a pair of pantyhose!

Back in Australia, nobody thinks box jellyfish are great, especially Aussie lifeguards. Anybody who enters the water here needs to wear something to protect themselves from the jellyfish's deadly tentacles. It has to be lightweight, yet thick enough to prevent the millions of stinging cells from penetrating the skin. The solution is pantyhose! Only the number one animal in the countdown could get a macho Aussie lifeguard to wear pantyhose. That's why when it comes to venom, the box jellyfish really is The Most Extreme.

For More Information

Anna Clairborne, *Octopuses.* Chicago: Raintree, 2004.

Ginjer L. Clarke, *Platypus!* New York: Random House, 2004.

Margery Facklam, *What's the Buzz? The Secret Life of Bees.* Austin, TX: Raintree Steck-Vaughn, 2001.

Janet Halfmann, *Scorpions.* San Diego: KidHaven Press, 2002.

Kris Hirschman, *The Octopus.* San Diego: KidHaven Press, 2003.

Bobbie Kalman, *The Life Cycle of a Honeybee.* New York: Crabtree, 2004.

David M. Nieves, *Reptiles Up Close.* Kansas City, MO: Reptile Education & Research, 1999.

Adele D. Richardson, *Scorpions.* Mankato, MN: Capstone Press, 2002.

Sharon Sharth, *Jellyfish.* Chanhassen, MN: Child's World, 2001.

Glossary

anaphylactic shock: a severe allergic reaction

antivenin: the antidote to a venom

apitherapy: the use of bee stings for the treatments of certain conditions

bacteria: microorganisms that can cause illness

biologist: a scientist who studies living organisms

enzymes: protein produced by living cells that help certain biological processes

keratin: fibrous proteins that form nails and hair

molecules: the smallest particles of a substance

neurotoxin: a poison that damages the nervous system

poisonous: a substance that injures or kills

venom: a poison produced by some animals and insects

venomous: an animal or insect that produces venom

Index